# The Magic of Pollinators

 Written by Gwen Petreman

Illustrated by Andrea Wray

Order this book online at www.trafford.com
or email orders@trafford.com

Most Trafford titles are also available at major online book retailers.

 www.trafford.com

**North America & international**
toll-free:  844 688 6899 (USA & Canada)
fax: 812 355 4082

Our mission is to efficiently provide the world's finest, most comprehensive book publishing service, enabling every author to experience success. To find out how to publish your book, your way, and have it available worldwide, visit us online at www.trafford.com

ISBN: 978-1-6987-0560-6 (sc)
ISBN: 978-1-6987-0559-0 (e)

Print information available on the last page.

Trafford rev.  02/13/2021

# Table of Contents

# What is pollination?

## HOW DO PLANTS MAKE NEW PLANTS?

For most plants, in order to make new plants, they need pollen grains from the male anther in the flower to be transferred to the female stigma found in the blossoms.

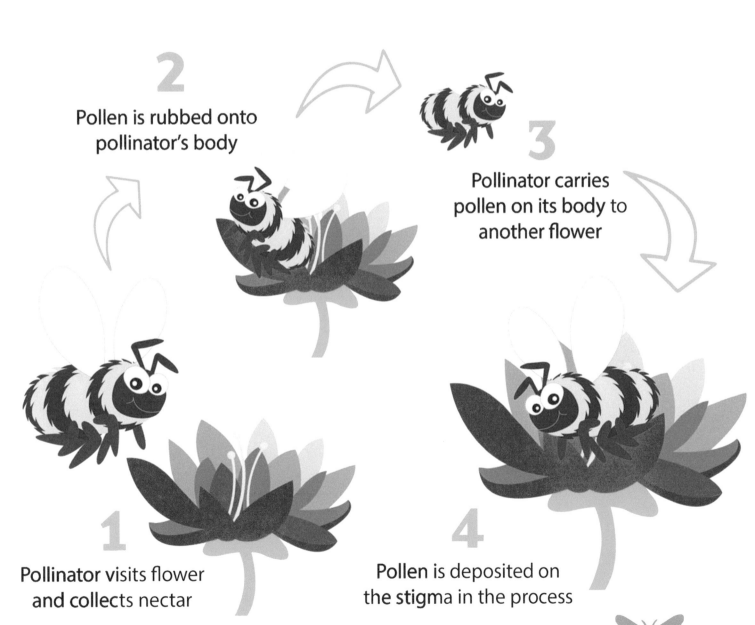

**2** Pollen is rubbed onto pollinator's body

**3** Pollinator carries pollen on its body to another flower

**1** Pollinator visits flower and collects nectar

**4** Pollen is deposited on the stigma in the process

# IS THERE MORE THAN ONE KIND OF POLLINATION?

Yes! There are two different types of pollination.

## 1. What is self-pollination?

Self-pollination occurs in the same plant.

The pollen grains are transferred from the male anther to the female stigma in the same flower.

Apricots, barley, beets, chard, coconuts, corn, millet, oats, pecans, pistachios, potatoes, rice, rye, spinach, tomatoes, walnuts, and wheat do not need pollinators as they are mostly pollinated by the wind.

## 2. What is cross-pollination?

In cross-pollination the pollen grains are transferred from the female anther of one plant to the male stigma of another plant.

Most of our flowering plants and most of our food crops need pollinators like bees to pollinate the flowers.

There are approximately 1, 000 plants grown for food like strawberries, for drinks like coffee, for spices like cilantro, and for fibres like cotton that need pollinators.

## Who are the pollinating agents?

Mammals, reptiles, birds, insects, and the wind that transfer the pollen grains from flower to flower are called pollinating agents.

Most pollinators are tiny.

But their importance is mighty!

Their job is to pollinate over 450, 000 species of plants!

Do you like sunflower seeds, apples, oranges, mangos, strawberries, almonds, and chocolate?

Do you like vanilla ice cream topped with strawberries and slivers of chocolate?

My mouth is watering for a bowl right now! Yum! Yum!

I hate to break the news to you but ... if our pollinators disappear you will no longer be able to enjoy your favourite dessert.

Cacao plants give us chocolate - m-m-m-m chocolate is my favourite.

Did you know that chocolate is actually a vegetable?

So next time your mom tells you to eat more veggies tell her, "Give me more chocolate, please!"

Would you believe that there are over 200, 000 different kinds of pollinators , but there is only one that is able to pollinate cacao plants?

The flowers on cacao plants are very tiny.

A very tiny fly called a midge is the only insect small enough to climb inside the small white flowers of cacao plants.

So you can see, even the tiniest insect plays a very important role in pollinating flowers.

# 1. INSECTS: THE MOST IMPORTANT POLLINATING AGENTS

## Honey Bees – number one pollinators

Most of the flowers (90%) in the world are pollinated by insects such as bees, beetles, moths, and flies.

Honey bees fly from flower to flower collecting nectar which they turn into honey.

Pollen grains attach to the honey bees' hind legs.

We refer to these collections of pollen as "pollen baskets".

Do you like apples?

Most people love the sweet taste of juicy apples.

Honey bees pollinate most apple orchards.

The owners of the apple orchards pay bee keepers to rent their hives.

After thousands of bees pollinate the apple blossoms, they turn into sweet, juicy apples.

## Squash Bees – love pumpkins

Did you know that if a tiny unimportant- looking bee called a squash bee disappeared, so will all the pumpkins in the whole world?

Squash bees are the only insects that will visit the flowers of pumpkins!

So thank the tiny squash bee next time you have fun carving a jack-o'-lantern!

Bumblebees are master pollinators!

The blossoms of blueberries are bell shaped with deep throats.

The tongues of bumblebees are nice and long so they can easily reach deep into a flower.

Their bodies are fat and furry.

Pollen easily gets stuck on their furry bodies.

Do you know what else makes them master pollinators?

Honey bees stay put in their hives if it's cloudy and rainy.

Bumblebees make honey bees look wimpy!

They will venture out in search of sweet nectar even on rainy days.

Are you ready to hear something gross about bumblebees? Bumblebees will actually eat the poop of other bumblebees!

Would you believe poop actually protects them from getting harmful parasites?

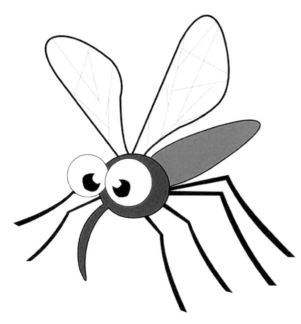

## Mosquitoes – pesky but ...

When you think of a mosquito you probably think of a pesky pest that will sting you and suck your blood! Right?

Actually the only mosquito that will suck your blood is a female mosquito.

And she only sucks your blood when she is ready to lay eggs.

Mosquitoes' favourite food is actually sweet nectar.

Mosquitoes pollinate orchid flowers that are able to grow right out of the branches of trees in tropical countries.

Do you like vanilla ice cream?

Guess what?

Vanilla comes from orchid flowers.

So next time you enjoy a vanilla ice cream, thank a pesky mosquito!

## Wasps – they will sting you but...

In late summer you probably become quite annoyed when uninvited wasps will readily try to make your sweet drink theirs.

And if you try to brush them aside, they have a nasty sting waiting for you in their stripy rear end.

If you thought that wasps are annoying, useless insects think again - they are so much more!

During the summer they need protein, so they search for aphids, flies, and caterpillars on all kinds of veggies.

Gardeners hate aphids and they especially hate caterpillars.

Caterpillars love leafy veggies!

Often when gardeners are ready to pick their veggies they find the veggie leaves riddled with holes made by hungry caterpillars.

Lucky for gardeners, wasps will readily eat caterpillars all summer long.

But, they actually  only eat a few of the caterpillars.

Can you guess what happens to most of the caterpillars?

Adult wasps have very important jobs.

Their job is to make sure that their hungry baby siblings are fed.

So the adults wasps feed caterpillars to the baby siblings.

In return the baby siblings secrete a sugary drink.

This sugary secretion is readily slurped up by the adult wasps.

When fall arrives, the baby siblings have become adults and no longer need to be fed.

As a result the adult wasps are no longer getting sugary drinks, so they look everywhere for something sweet.

Not only do they look for something sweet at your outdoor picnic, but they will also look for sweet nectar from flowers.

It turns out in the fall, wasps can be just as amazing as bees at pollinating flowers!

## Beetles – don't get grossed out

Beetles do not look for nectar like bees.

They are actually looking for pollen.

Beetles pollinate flowers quite differently from other pollinators.

It is kind of gross! Are you ready? Here goes ...

First, they eat parts of the flower.

Then they poop inside the flower.

Finally, they roll around in the poopy pollen. Triple yuck!

Some flowers pollinated by beetles are golden rod, magnolias, and pond lilies.

# 2. BIRDS ARE IMPORTANT POLLINATING AGENTS

## Hummingbirds – master acrobats

Hummingbirds are not only dazzling, but they are very special kinds of pollinators.

Due to their long beaks they are able to pollinate blossoms that no other pollinators can!

Why? Some flowers have very deep throats.

The throats are so deep that bees and other pollinating insects simply cannot reach the nectar.

Tiny pollen grains stick to their long sword-like beaks or their tiny foreheads.

Have you ever seen a hummingbird walk?

Their feet are too tiny for walking.

That is good news for flowers!

Hummingbirds cause no damage to flowers, as they just hover like helicopters, while they gently slip their beaks into deep-throated flowers.

Hummingbirds are multi-talented.

If they could participate in the Olympics, they would be awarded gold for their acrobatic-flying skills.

They cannot only fly forward, but they can also fly backward, sideways, and straight up in the air.

Pretty astounding, right!

But, wait there is more.

As they dart from flower to flower searching for nectar and insects, they can actually do backward somersaults!

So, even hummingbirds like to have fun.

If that is not enough expertise for one bird, they possess even more record-breaking skills!

These tiny "flying jewels" can fly up to 95 kilometres per hour!

The ruby -throated hummingbirds' migration is quite astounding! These tiny birds migrate all alone and never in flocks. They fly over 4,000 kilometres (2,485 miles), all the way from Canada to Central America.

How brave of them
to fly over 800 km
(500 miles) for up to
22 hours non-stop
over the
open waters
of the Gulf
of Mexico!

Just because
hummingbirds
are the tiniest of
all bird species,
do not believe for
a single second
that they are weak
and helpless!

Believe it or not, if other
birds invade hummingbird
territory, these tiny birds will readily
attack blue jays, crows, and even
sharp-beaked hawks.

What do you call a flock of hummingbirds?

Next time, you see a group of hummingbirds, impress
your friends by calling them a shimmer of hummingbirds.

CANADA

CENTRAL
AMERICA

# 3. EVEN SOME VERTEBRATES ARE POLLINATING AGENTS

Some flowering plants are pollinated by kinkajous, monkeys, lemurs, possums, lizards, and even rodents like rats.

The honey possum is a tiny marsupial who feeds on the nectar of all kinds of flowering plants in Australia.

When the ruffled lemurs of Madagascar reach into the flowers of the traveler's palm tree, they get pollen all over their snouts.

Rats like the nectar of flowers and as they go from flower to flower they help with pollination.

While the day time pollinators sleep, nocturnal pollinators will pollinate flowers all night long.

Who are the nighttime pollinators you might ask?

Fruit bats pollinate plants that flower at nighttime.

Would you believe that there are over 300 different food producing plants that need fruit bats to pollinate them?

Do you like mangos, dates, and cashew nuts?

They all need fruit bats to pollinate them!

Moths also pollinate flowers at night.

Night moths will pollinate moonflowers, evening primrose, nicotiana, and morning glories.

## 4. EVEN HUMANS CAN BE POLLINATING AGENTS

If you shake a tomato plant, you can help with self-pollination.

Or you can get a cotton swab to collect pollen and move it to another flower.

# How can I help pollinators in my neighbourhood?

- Ask your parents to create a Pollinator Patch in your garden.

Check the chart for some native plants grown in North America that attract pollinators.

Bee Balm

Cup Plant

Black-Eyed Susan

Common Milkweed

Cone Flower

Turtlehead

Butterfly Weed

Ironweed

When you spy a moth, butterfly, bee or hummingbird flitting from flower to flower say, "Thank-you!"

If you suddenly see a milkweed growing in your garden DO NOT PULL IT OUT! Why you might ask.

Monarch butterflies lay their eggs on milkweed leaves, but the Monarch caterpillars can eat no other plants but milkweed leaves. If the milkweed plants disappear, so will the Monarch butterflies.

Place a butterfly house or cedar bee house in your backyard.

Find out how your town can become an official Bee City.

Ask your parents not to use pesticides on flowers as they will not only kill pests, but they also kill our precious pollinators.

## True or false?

**1.** Even a tiger can help pollinate flowers. T or F

**2.** Pollinating agents transfer pollen grains from flower to flower. T or F

**3.** A midge is the only insect that will pollinate the flowers of orange trees. T or F

**4.** There are over 300 different food producing plants pollinated by fruit bats. T or F

**5.** Some honey bees are nighttime pollinators. T or F

**6.** Hummingbirds are really great at pollinating deep-throated flowers. T or F

**7.** If tiny midges disappear, we would not be able to eat real chocolate. T or F

**8.** Humans can actually pollinate flowers. T or F

**9.** Even rats can be pollinating agents. T or F

**10.** The best pollinating agents are dogs and cats. T or F

## Find 2 pollinators in each line

**1.** emnmidgescxzkbutterfliestrasradbutreflysklpmigsx

**2.** hratsaneyboeplhoneybeesdshpyqhaneybeajratsaph

**3.** mophjkldsgmosquitoesmathsbvcdhpnomothspkjhlx

**4.** frulkhfruitbadsmhumanslghbadsghkzxfruit batsdmnj

**5.** plkmnjhbridsmklpwebirdsmbnjhbumblebeesbnlkddf

Draw 3 of your favourite pollinators and label each one

## Riddles

**1.** I am a pollinator. Without me you would not be able to eat chocolate.

**2.** I am a pollinator. I have a long beak. I am a great flyer, but I cannot walk.

**3.** I am a pollinator. I am the only mammal that can fly. I pollinate mangos.

**4.** I am a pollinator. I pollinate more flowers than any other pollinator. I collect nectar which I turn into honey.

**5.** I am a pollinator. I am an insect. I pollinate flowers at nighttime.

## Draw a hummingbird

Label its body parts.

wings, feet, legs, throat, beak, head, body, tail, chin, eye

## Draw a butterfly

Label its body parts.

head, thorax, abdomen, antennae, wings, 6 legs, proboscis, wing veins, forewings, hindwings

## Design a perfect pollinator

Give it a name. Label its body parts. Write a story about it.

## Interview a pollinator

Pretend you are a News Reporter. List 5 questions you would ask a hummingbird. Then try to answer the questions.

## Figure out the math problem

Then draw the correct answers.

(12–9) rats , (18–14) honey bees, (16–13) moths,
(14 –12) hummingbirds

## Answer questions from the book

**1.** What is a pollinator?

**2.** How do plants make new plants?

**3.** What is self-pollination?

**4.** What is cross-pollination?

**5.** How many plants are grown for food?

**6.** How many different species of plants are pollinated by pollinators?

**7.** Is chocolate a fruit or a vegetable?

**8.** What is a "pollen basket"?

**9.** How do honey bees help to grow apples?

**10.** Why is a squash bee important?

**11.** Which insects are master pollinators?

**12.** Why do bumblebees eat the poop of other bumblebees?

**13.** What do honey bees do on cloudy and rainy days?

**14.** Why should you thank a pesky mosquito for your vanilla ice cream?

**15.** Why are you pestered mainly by wasps in the fall?

**16.** Which insect likes to roll around in pollen covered in poop?

**17.** Why are hummingbirds special pollinators?

**18.** What do fruit bats do at nighttime?

**19.** Name three food items that fruit bats pollinate?

**20.** Why are milkweed plants important to Monarch butterflies?

Printed in the United States
by Baker & Taylor Publisher Services